Dear Parents:

Congratulations! Your child is taking the first steps on an exciting journey. The destination? Independent reading!

STEP INTO READING® will help your child get there. The program offers five steps to reading success. Each step includes fun stories and colorful art or photographs. In addition to original fiction and books with favorite characters, there are Step into Reading Non-Fiction Readers, Phonics Readers and Boxed Sets, Sticker Readers, and Comic Readers—a complete literacy program with something to interest every child.

Learning to Read, Step by Step!

Ready to Read   Preschool–Kindergarten
• big type and easy words • rhyme and rhythm • picture clues
For children who know the alphabet and are eager to begin reading.

Reading with Help   Preschool–Grade 1
• basic vocabulary • short sentences • simple stories
For children who recognize familiar words and sound out new words with help.

Reading on Your Own   Grades 1–3
• engaging characters • easy-to-follow plots • popular topics
For children who are ready to read on their own.

Reading Paragraphs   Grades 2–3
• challenging vocabulary • short paragraphs • exciting stories
For newly independent readers who read simple sentences with confidence.

Ready for Chapters   Grades 2–4
• chapters • longer paragraphs • full-color art
For children who want to take the plunge into chapter books but still like colorful pictures.

STEP INTO READING® is designed to give every child a successful reading experience. The grade levels are only guides; children will progress through the steps at their own speed, developing confidence in their reading.

Remember, a lifetime love of reading starts with a single step!

RHUS33531

 Published in the United States by Random House Children's Books, a division of Random House LLC, 1745 Broadway, New York, NY 10019, and in Canada by Random House of Canada Limited, Toronto, Penguin Random House Companies.

Visit us on the Web!
StepIntoReading.com
randomhousekids.com
dckids.kidswb.com

Educators and librarians, for a variety of teaching tools, visit us at RHTeachersLibrarians.com

ISBN 978-0-553-50808-6 (trade) – ISBN 978-0-553-50809-3 (lib. bdg.)
ISBN 978-0-553-50810-9 (ebook)

Printed in the United States of America

10 9 8 7 6 5 4 3 2 1

STEP 2 READING WITH HELP

STEP INTO READING®

DC SUPER FRIENDS™

BATMAN'S HERO FILES

by Billy Wrecks
illustrated by Erik Doescher

Random House New York

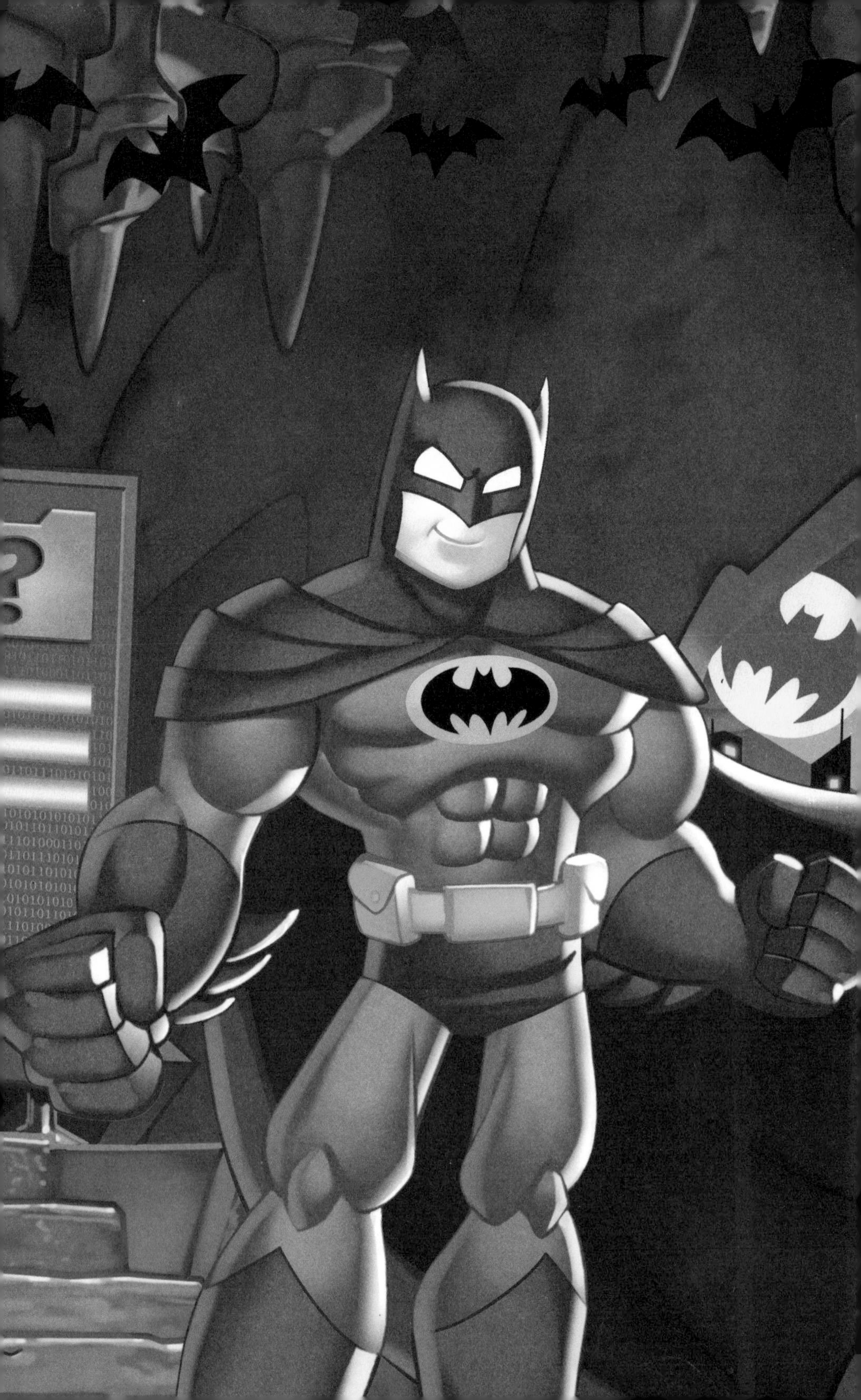

Batman

The Super Friends are
the world's finest heroes!
Batman keeps files
on all the heroes.
He knows their powers
and awesome skills.

Superman

Superman has super-strength, and he is indestructible.

He has powerful
heat vision,
and he can fly
at amazing speed—
even in space!

Wonder Woman

Bad guys have
to tell the truth
when Wonder Woman
catches them
in her magic lasso.

She is strong and fast.
She can deflect any attack
with her silver bracelets!

Green Lantern

Green Lantern uses
his power ring to fly
and create force fields.

He can make anything
that he imagines
with his power ring.
He uses it to protect
Earth from alien threats.

Green Arrow

Green Arrow fights crime with a bow and arrow.

He uses many kinds
of arrows to bring down
the bad guys.

He always hits his target!

The Flash

The Flash is
the Fastest Man Alive!

He can outrun
a speeding train,
run up the side
of a building,
and even run on water!

Cyborg

Cyborg is part man
and part machine.

He can form a blaster
and other weapons
with his robot body.

He is also super-smart,
so he can out-think
any foe!

Batgirl

Batgirl is swift and silent
when she sneaks up
on the bad guys.

She uses a Utility Belt
that is packed
with everything
she needs to fight crime.

Aquaman

Aquaman lives underwater.

He can talk to fish
and other sea creatures.
Aquaman dives deep
to protect the world's
oceans and seas!

Batman

Batman is
the Dark Knight.
He uses brains, brawn,
and detective skills
to fight every foe.

By knowing all about
the Super Friends' powers,
he knows who can
stop the villains . . .

. . . and keep the world safe.

Go, Super Friends!